ON BEYOND ZEBRA

By
Dr. Seuss

RANDOM HOUSE · NEW YORK

BOOKS BY DR. SEUSS

And to Think That I Saw It on Mulberry Street
The 500 Hats of Bartholomew Cubbins
The King's Stilts
Horton Hatches the Egg
McElligot's Pool
Thidwick The Big-Hearted Moose
Bartholomew and the Oobleck
If I Ran the Zoo
Scrambled Eggs Super
Horton Hears a Who
On Beyond Zebra
If I Ran the Circus
How the Grinch Stole Christmas
Yertle the Turtle and Other Stories
Happy Birthday to You
The Sneetches and Other Stories
Dr. Seuss's Sleep Book
I Had Trouble in Getting to Solla Sollew
The Cat in the Hat Songbook
I Can Lick 30 Tigers Today and Other Stories
The Lorax
Did I Ever Tell You How Lucky You Are?
Hunches in Bunches
The Butter Battle Book

BEGINNER BOOKS

The Cat in the Hat
The Cat in the Hat Comes Back
One Fish Two Fish Red Fish Blue Fish
Green Eggs and Ham
Hop on Pop
Dr. Seuss's ABC
Fox in Socks
The Foot Book
My Book About Me
Mr. Brown Can Moo! Can You?
Marvin K. Mooney, Will You Please Go Now?
The Shape of Me and Other Stuff
There's A Wocket in My Pocket
Great Day for Up
Oh, The Thinks You Can Think
The Cat's Quizzer
I Can Read With My Eyes Shut
Oh Say Can You Say?

This title was originally catalogued by the Library of Congress as follows:
Geisel, Theodor Seuss. On beyond zebra, by Dr. Seuss [pseud.] New York, Random House [1955] I. Title.
PZ8.3.G276On   55-9321
ISBN: 0-394-80084-2 (trade hardcover)   0-394-90084-7 (library binding)   0-394-84541-2 (trade paperback)

Manufactured in the United States of America   3 4 5 6 7 8 9 0

To Helen

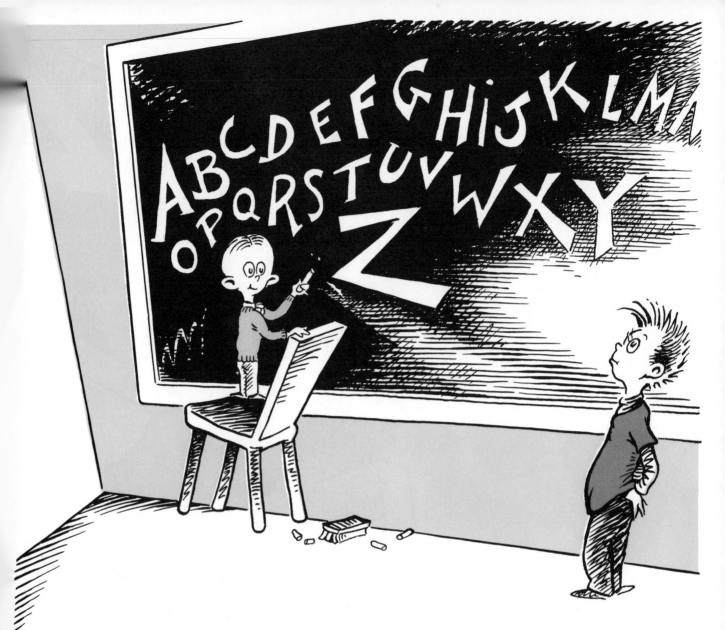

Said Conrad Cornelius o'Donald o'Dell,
My very young friend who is learning to spell:
"The A is for Ape. And the B is for Bear.
"The C is for Camel. The H is for Hare.
"The M is for Mouse. And the R is for Rat.
"I know *all* the twenty-six letters like that . . .

"...through to Z is for Zebra. I know them all well."
Said Conrad Cornelius o'Donald o'Dell.
"So now I know everything *any*one knows
"From beginning to end. From the start to the close.
"Because Z is as far as the alphabet goes."

Then he almost fell flat on his face on the floor
When I picked up the chalk and drew one letter more!
A letter he never had dreamed of before!
And I said, "*You* can stop, if you want, with the Z
"Because most people stop with the Z
"*But not me!*

"In the places I go there are things that I see
"That I *never* could spell if I stopped with the Z.
"I'm telling you this 'cause you're one of my friends.
"*My* alphabet starts where *your* alphabet ends!

My alphabet starts with this letter called YUZZ.
It's the letter I use to spell Yuzz-a-ma-Tuzz.
You'll be sort of surprised what there is to be found
Once you go beyond Z and start poking around!

So, on beyond Zebra!
Explore!
Like Columbus!
Discover new letters!
Like WUM is for Wumbus,
My high-spouting whale who lives high on a hill
And who never comes down 'til it's time to refill.
So, on beyond Z! It's high time you were shown
That you really *don't* know all there is to be known.

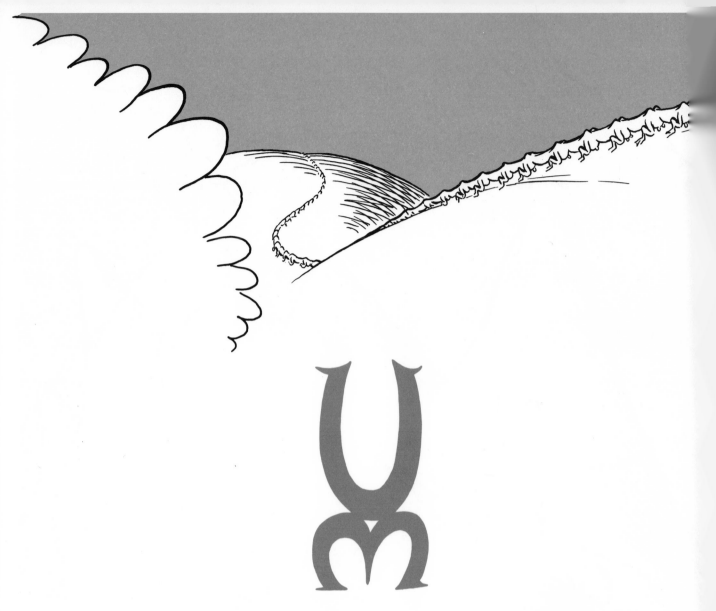

Then just step a step further past Wum is for Wumbus
And there you'll find UM. And the Um is for Umbus
A sort of a Cow, with one head and one tail,
But to milk this great cow you need more than one pail!
She has ninety-eight faucets that give milk quite nicely.
Perhaps ninety-nine. I forget just precisely.
And, boy! She is something *most* people don't see
Because most people stop at the Z
But not me!

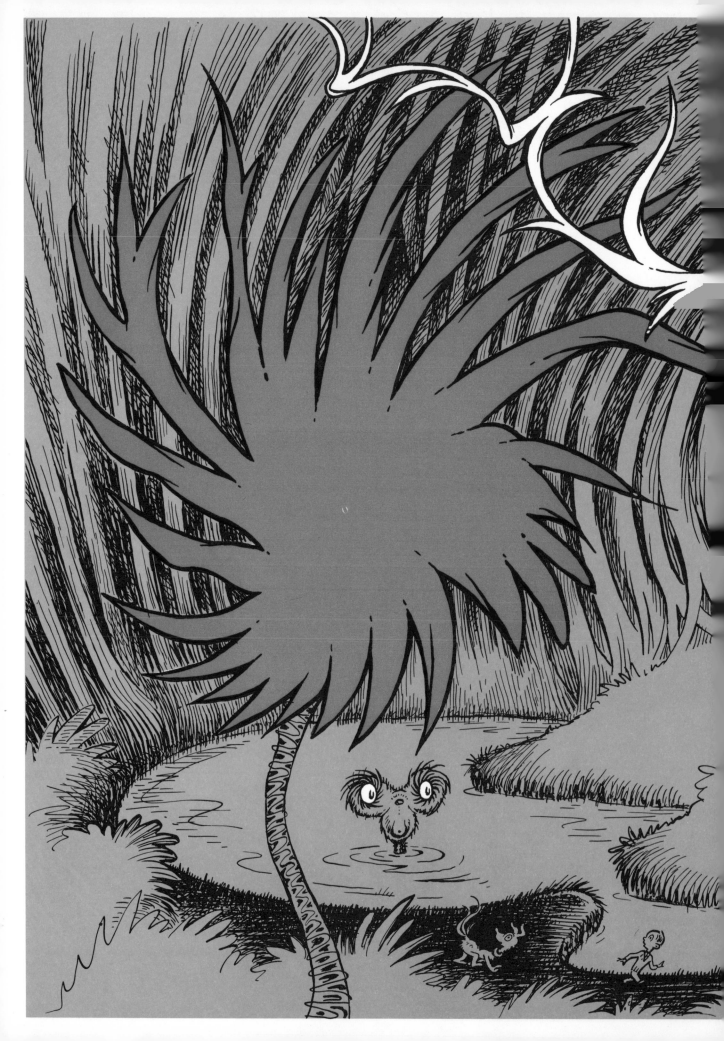

I ramble, I scramble through swampf and through swumpf
Where the letters get better. Like letters like HUMPF.
There's a real handy letter.
What's handy about it ...?
You just can't spell Humpf-Humpf-a-Dumpfer without it.

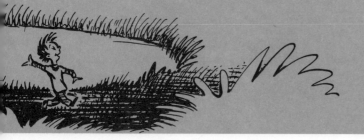

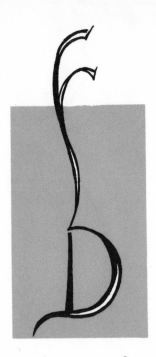

If you stay home with Zebra,
You're stuck in a rut.
But on beyond Zebra,
You're anything but!

Why, I know a fine fancy letter called FUDDLE.
I use it in spelling Miss Fuddle-dee-Duddle.
And, oh! What a bird-of-a-bird-of-a-bird-of!
Her tail is the longest that's ever been heard of.
So long and so fancy she'd be in a fix
If she didn't have helpers. It takes about six
To tag along, hoisting Miss Fuddle-dee-Duddle's
Wonderful tail out of muddle-dee-puddles.

And GLIKK is for Glikker who lives in wild weeds
And spends his time juggling fresh cinnamon seeds
Which he's usually able to find in great number
Excepting, of course, in the month of SeptUmber
When cinnamon seeds *aren't* around in great number.
So *that* month he juggles with seeds of cucumber.

And NUH is the letter I use to spell Nutches
Who live in small caves, known as Nitches, for hutches.
These Nutches have troubles, the biggest of which is
The fact there are many more Nutches than Nitches.
Each Nutch in a Nitch knows that some other Nutch
Would like to move into his Nitch very much.
So each Nutch in a Nitch has to watch that small Nitch
Or Nutches who haven't got Nitches will snitch.

Then we go on to SNEE. And the SNEE is for Sneedle
A terrible kind of ferocious mos-keedle
Whose hum-dinger stinger is sharp as a needle.

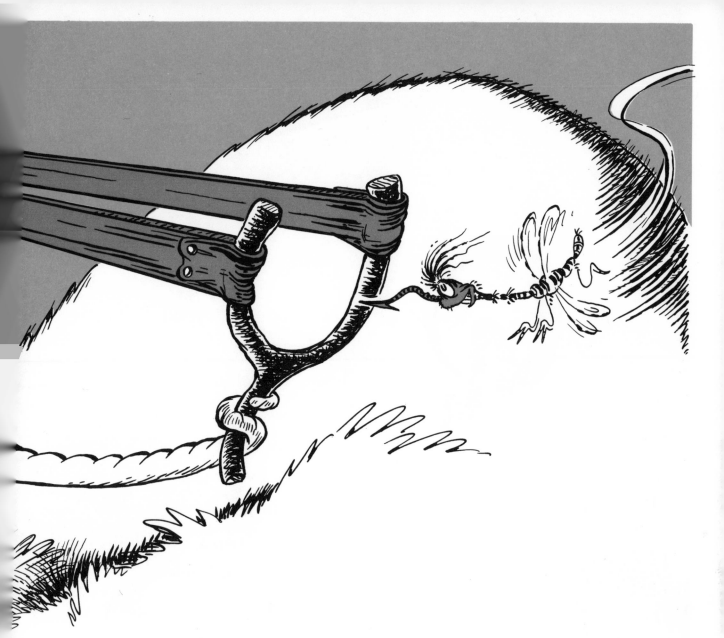

The Sneedle's too tough to be killed with a smack
So he has to be hunted on elephant back
And your eyes and the elephant's have to be keen
And you have to aim fast and you have to hit clean
And the bullet you shoot is a stale navy bean
That you've dunked for three weeks in old sour kerosene
Which is awfully hard work. So it's easy to see
Why most people stop at the Z. *But not me!*

When you go beyond Zebra,
Who knows..?
There's no telling
What wonderful things
You might find yourself spelling!
Like QUAN is for Quandary, who lives on a shelf
In a hole in the ocean alone by himself
And he worries, each day, from the dawn's early light
And he worries, just worries, far into the night.
He just stands there and worries. He simply can't stop...
Is his top-side his bottom? Or bottom-side top?

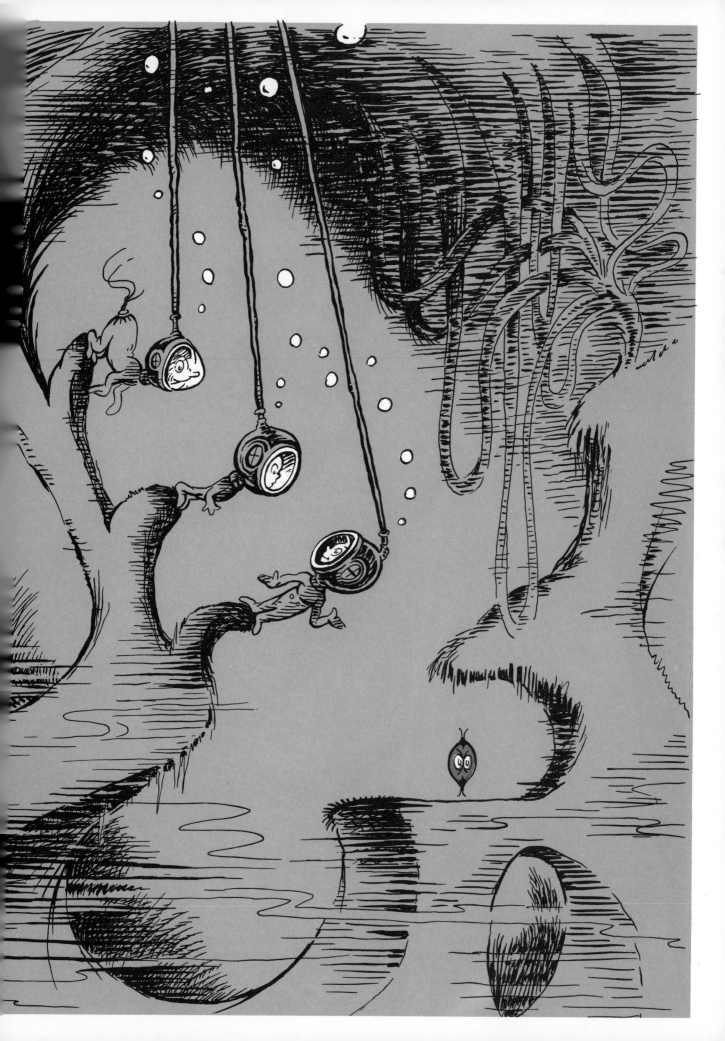

And THNAD is for Thnadners
And oh, are they sad, oh!
The big one, you see, has the smaller one's shadow.
The shadow the *small* Thnadner has should be *his*.
I don't understand it, but that's how it is.
A terrible mix-up in shadows! Gee-Whizz!

And SPAZZ is a letter I use to spell Spazzim
A beast who belongs to the Nazzim of Bazzim.
Handy for traveling. That's why he has 'im.
More easy to pack than a suitcase or grip,
Those horns carry all that he needs on a trip:
A thread and a needle for mending his socks,
His tooth brush,
A cup,
And two three-handed clocks.
And his velvet umbrella,
His vegetable chopper,
And also his gold-plated popping-corn popper
And a grasshopper cage for his favorite grass hopper.

And FLOOB is for Floob-Boober-Bab-Boober-Bubs
Who bounce in the water like blubbery tubs.
They're no good to eat.
You can't cook 'em like steaks.
But they're handy in crossing small oceans and lakes.

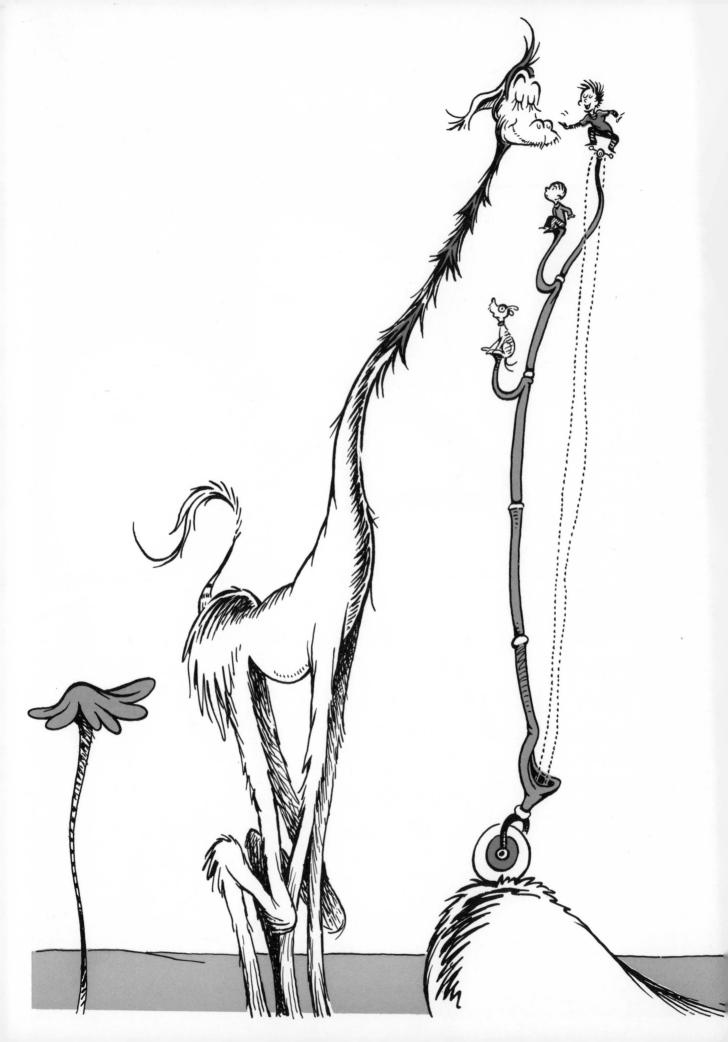

And ZATZ is the letter I use to spell Zatz-it
Whose nose is so high that 'most nobody pats it
And patting his lonely old nose is the least
That a fellow could do for this fine friendly beast
So, to get there and do it, I built an invention:
The Three-Seater Zatz-it Nose-Patting Extension.
    If *you* try to drive one,
            You'll certainly see
                Why most people stop at the Z
                        But not me!

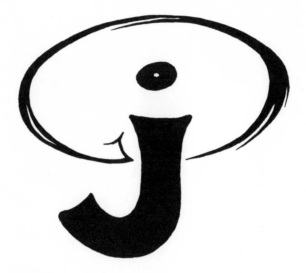

And JOGG is my letter for spelling Jogg-oons
Who doodle around in the far desert dunes
Just doodle around, crooning very sad tunes
About peppermint, peanuts and pebbles and prunes
And paint pots, and polka dots, pin heads and pigs
And their grandmother's grandfather's step-sister's wigs.

So you see!
There's no end
To the things you might know,
Depending how far beyond Zebra you go!

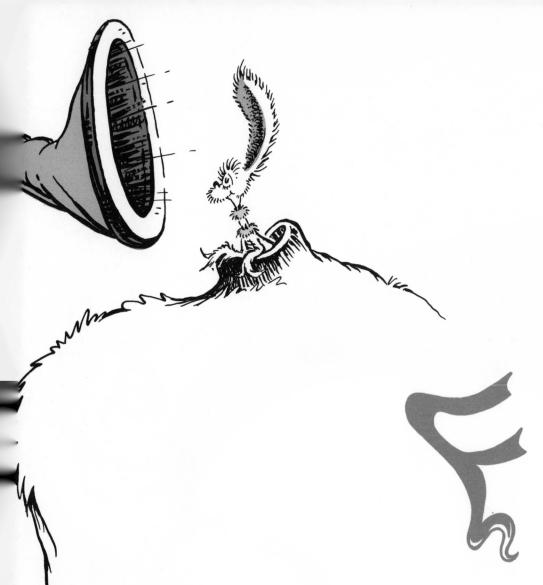

I've a letter called FLUNN. And the FLUNN is for Flunnel
A softish nice fellow who hides in a tunnel.
He *only* comes out of his hole, I'm afraid,
When the right kind of softish nice music is played
On a kind of a hunting horn called the o'Grunth.
And to learn how to play it takes month after month
Of practising, practising. Isn't much fun-th.
And, besides, it's quite heavy. Weighs almost a tun-th.
That's why few people bother to play the o'Grunth
So the Flunnel's been out of his tunnel just one-th.

And 'way, 'way past Z is a letter called ITCH
And the ITCH is for Itch-a-pods, animals which
Race around back and forth, forth and back, through the air
On a very high sidewalk between HERE and THERE.
They're afraid to stay THERE. They're afraid to stay HERE.
They think THERE is too Far. They think HERE is too NEAR.
And since HERE is too NEAR and out THERE is too FAR
They are too scared to roost where-so-ever they are.

There's a letter called YEKK. And the YEKK is for Yekko
Who howls in an underground grotto in Gekko.
These Yekkos love echoes, and this is their motto:
"For best Yekko echoes, try Gekko, our grotto!"

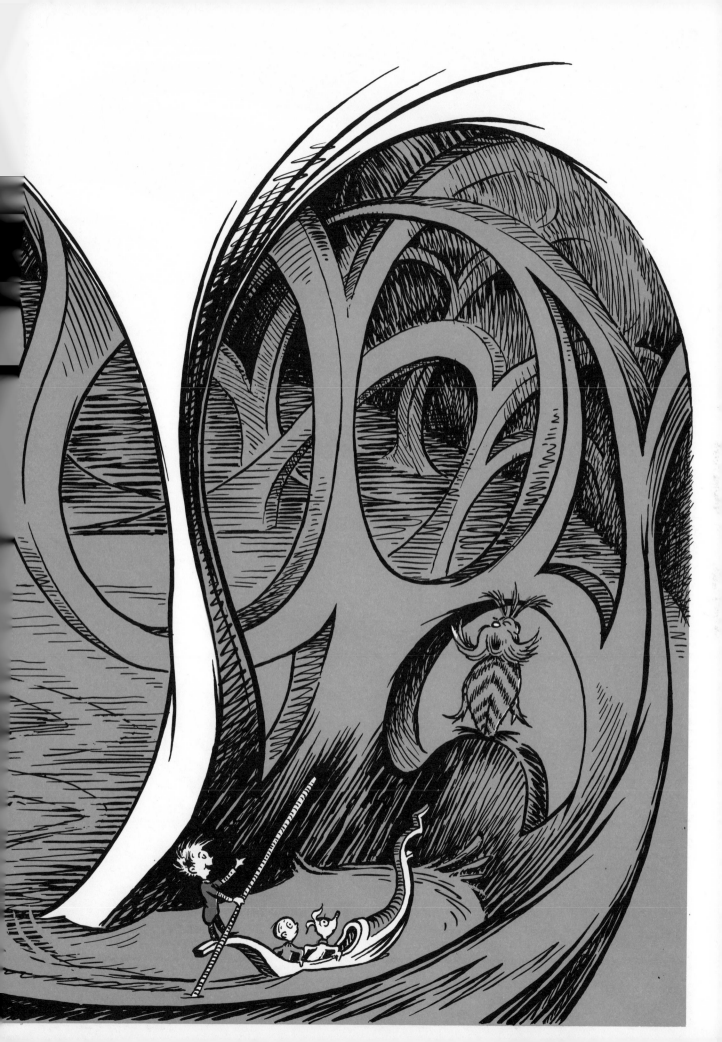

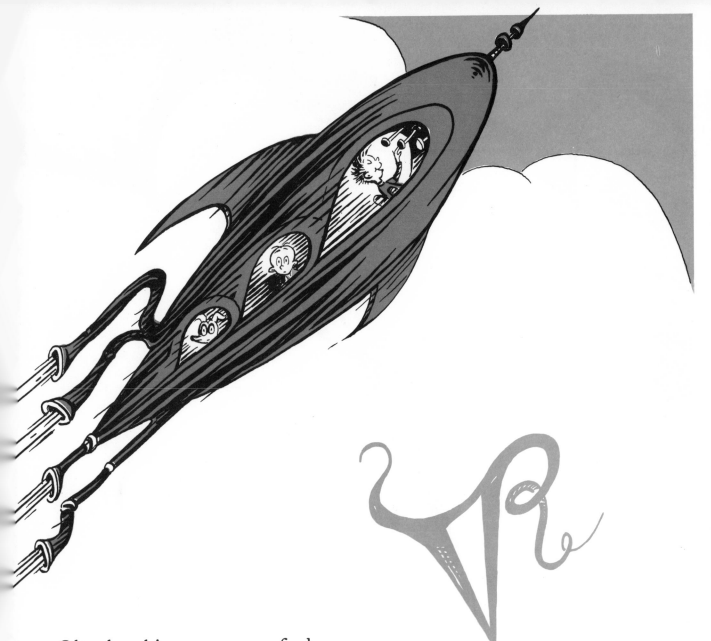

Oh, the things you can find
If you don't stay behind!
On a world near the sun live two brothers called VROOMS
Who, strangely enough, are built sort of like brooms
And they're stuck all alone up there high in the blue
And so, to kill time, just for something to do
Each one of these fellows takes turns with the other
In sweeping the dust off his world with his brother.

And *HI!* is my letter for High Gargel-orum.
For getting me places real fast, I'm all for 'em.
They puffle along and their brakes never squeak
And they run every hour every day of the week
From the town of North Nubb
To the town of East Ounce,
Making stops at West Bunglefield, Yupster and Jounce
And at Ipswich and Nipswich and, also, South Bounce
And another small town that's too hard to pronounce.

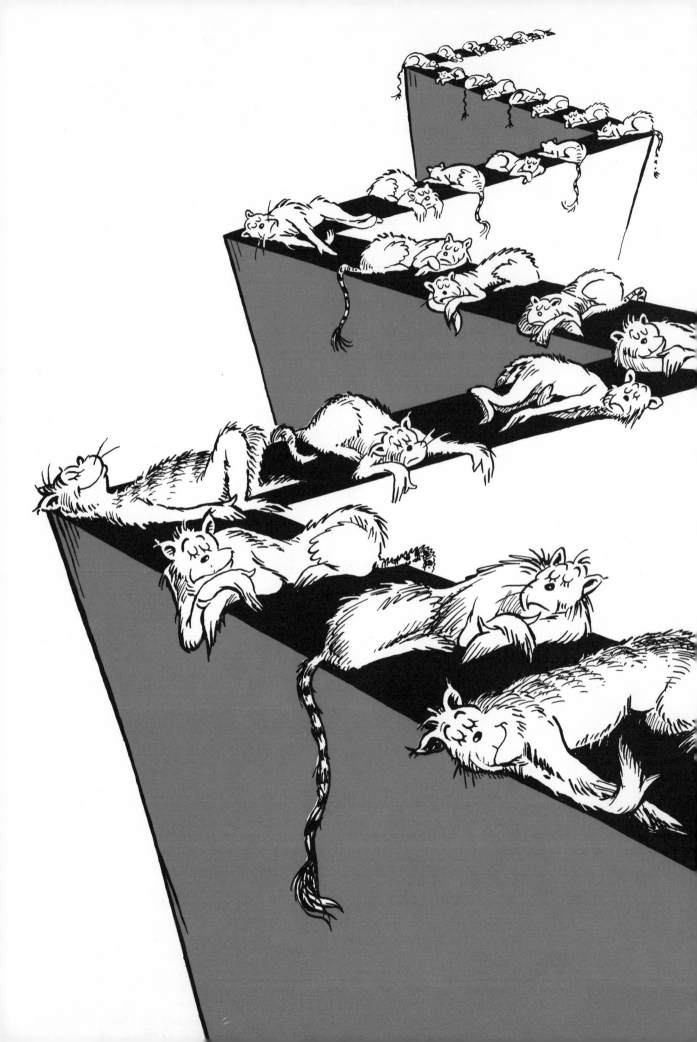

The places I took him!

I tried hard to tell

Young Conrad Cornelius o'Donald o'Dell

A few brand-new wonderful words he might spell.

I led him around and I tried hard to show

There are things beyond Z that most people don't know.

I took him past Zebra. As far as I could.

And I think, perhaps, maybe I did him some good...

Because, finally, he said:
   "This is really great stuff!
     "And I guess the old alphabet
          "ISN'T enough!"

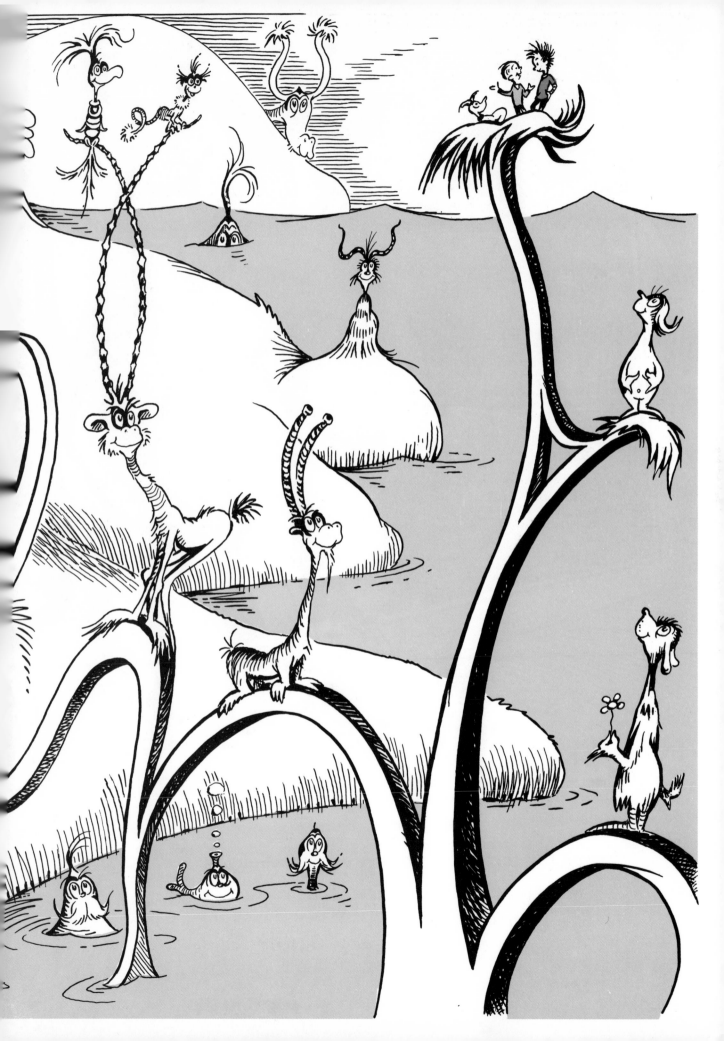

NOW the letters he uses are something to see!
Most people *still* stop at the Z...
But not HE!

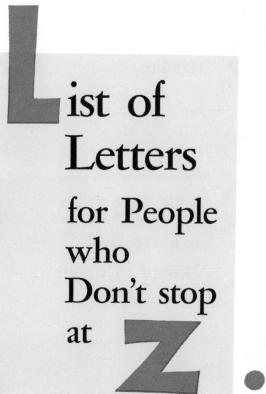

List of Letters for People who Don't stop at **Z**

YUZZ
is for
Yuzz-a-ma-Tuzz

GLIKK
is for
Glikker

WUM
is for
Wumbus

NUH
is for
Nutches

UM
is for
Umbus

SNEE
is for
Sneedle

HUMPF
is for Humpf-
Humpf-a-Dumpfer

QUAN
is for
Quandary

FUDDLE
is for Miss
Fuddle-dee-Duddle

THNAD
is for
Thnadner

SPAZZ
is for
Spazzim

ITCH
is for
Itch-a-pods

FLOOB
is for Floob-Boober
Bab-Boober-Bubs

YEKK
is for
Yekko

ZATZ
is for
Zatz-it

VROO
is for
Vrooms

JOGG
is for
Jogg-oons

HI!
is for
High Gargel-orum

FLUNN
is for
Flunnel

and ●●●➤

●●● what do YOU think
we should call this one, anyhow?